The Red Ribbon

A story of hope.

*Created by John Lasne and
Brains On Fire*

RED RIBBON WORKS!
KEEPING KIDS OFF DRUGS

D E D I C A T I O N

This storybook is dedicated to the memory of Enrique ("Kiki") Camarena,
a drug enforcement agent who gave his life fighting the war against drugs,
and is the inspiration for the Red Ribbon Celebration.
He showed that one person can make a difference.

The Red Ribbon is dedicated also to Kiki's mother, Dora, and his sister, Myrna,
who have continued his fight against drugs. It is through their partnership and friendship
that the magic of the Red Ribbon lives.

Based on a story by John Lasne
Illustrations by Greg Ramsey

Published by Woofgang Brand Development

Distributed by Red Ribbon Works to support grassroots prevention and Keeping Kids Off Drugs
PO Box 10203
Greenville, SC 29603-0203

First Printing

LIBRARY OF CONGRESS CATALOGING IN PUBLICATION DATA

The Red Ribbon.

ISBN 0-9642815-0-3

Library of Congress Catalog Card Number: 94-68021

Printed in Canada on Luna Matte 100 LB. from Island Paper Mills

FOREWORD

The Red Ribbon is an education and prevention story developed to reach children. Readers will discover a kingdom where an overwhelming sadness is conquered, not by the bravest knight or the most powerful wizard, but by those who join "hands and hearts" for the good of all. *The Red Ribbon* is an effective training tool for parents and teachers who wish to instill their children with values that will withstand the dangers of drugs.

Since its inception, the Red Ribbon storybook exemplifies the mission of all involved—Keeping Kids off Drugs.

The greatest gift to the future is drug-free youth. *The Red Ribbon* carries its simple, powerful message to children and adults everywhere: bright futures for all our children are in the hands and hearts of each of us.

For more information on Red Ribbon Works and drug prevention programs, contact GFP/Red Ribbon Works at 800-732-4099 or PO Box 10203, Greenville, SC 29603-0203 or visit our web site at www.redribbonworks.org.

ot long ago in a nearby land, a good king looked out over his kingdom. From high in the castle tower he could see everything — tall trees in the forests, beautiful gardens and farmlands, the crystal blue river and all of the people who lived and worked in the village below. One would think, with all of these beautiful things in sight, the King would be very happy, but he wasn't. Instead, the King was quite sad. All he could see when he looked out his window was a terrible sadness in his kingdom.

Because the people in the village were afraid, the King worried and worried, and the smile he once had turned into a big frown. The King knew if he didn't do something soon to stop the sadness, he and his kingdom might never be happy again.

So, the King sent royal messengers to find the wisest, most powerful people in all the land and invite them to the castle to help save the kingdom. He invited dukes and duchesses, princes and princesses, lords and scholars.

When they arrived, he gathered them all in a big room to tell them about the terrible sadness he could see from his window.

Help Wanted

If you are wise, powerful and free this weekend I need your help!
The King

1

My friends," he said, "the kingdom has great forests with many trees for wood. Yet, I see people who have no houses. The crystal river is full of fish and there are farms as far as the eye can see, yet I see many people who are hungry because they have no food. There are people from many nations with much to share, yet I see selfishness and fear. And the saddest thing of all," the King said as his frown grew even bigger,

"though I listen as hard as I can, I hear no children laughing. I can see no children playing. They stay in their homes, afraid to come outside.

"My friends, I need your help. You are my last hope. If we don't stop the sadness, it will soon destroy the kingdom."

The sounds of whispers filled the room as the guests tried hard to think of ways to help the King.

Your Majesty," someone cried, "perhaps you should send a brave knight to conquer this terrible sadness."

"Yes, yes!" agreed everyone. "Surely a brave knight could save the kingdom."

The King, sitting on his throne, just shook his head. "I have already tried that. I sent the mightiest knight in all the land to conquer the sadness. But it was too strong. My brave knight was defeated."

"I've got it!" exclaimed another guest. "Perhaps the kingdom is under an evil spell and a great wizard is needed to stop the sadness."

Again, everyone agreed. "Yes! Yes! Surely a wizard could save the kingdom."

Again the King shook his head. "I'm sorry, my friends, but you see I've tried that too. The sadness is not an evil spell. The wizard could not help me."

The King could see that even his wise and powerful friends had no ideas, and the frown on his face was now bigger than ever.

Suddenly, from the back of the room they heard a voice. "Your Majesty, I know how to conquer the sadness!"

Everyone grew very quiet and all eyes looked to the back of the room as a man stepped forward from the shadows. They all stared as he made his way to the front. He seemed a plain, ordinary man dressed in plain, ordinary clothes. Over his shoulder he carried a curious leather sack. It was brown and exceedingly large.

When the man reached the throne, he politely knelt before the King, who asked, "Do I know you, sir? Are you a prince or a duke or brave knight?"

Before the man could answer, a guest shouted, "He's a magician! Look! He's carrying a bag of tricks."

The King inquired, "Is that true? Are you a magician? Do you have magic that can heal my kingdom?"

The man smiled at the King. "Your Majesty, I'm not a duke, or a knight or a prince and I'm certainly no magician. I am just a simple weaver. I make cloth in the village below."

"A weaver?" marveled the King.

Everyone started whispering again. The King squinted as he studied the stranger. "How can *you* help me?" the King asked.

he man stood and explained, "Though I am not a king or a prince or a magician, I know of a great power that can stop the sadness. Gather everyone in the kingdom and meet me at the castle gates as the sun rises. Do exactly as I say and the kingdom will be saved."

A guest cried, "This man is just a weaver from the village. What power could he have that we do not know about? After all, we are the wisest most powerful people in the land."

"There!" another guest quickly pointed to the weaver's sack.

"The magic power must be in that big brown sack." The room quieted once again. The King leaned forward, peered at the sack and asked the weaver, "Is the power to defeat the sadness in the leather sack you carry?"

The weaver thought for a moment, and then slowly leaned toward the King until their noses nearly touched. "As I said before, Your Majesty, gather everyone in the kingdom, meet me at sunrise, and you shall see."

The King sat back in his throne and scratched his head. "This, I have not tried," he thought. "This weaver's magic may be my only hope."

Then he rose to his feet and commanded, "Send the royal messengers! We will meet at sunrise and do as the weaver says."

Wasting no time, the messengers rode throughout the land telling everyone about the weaver and his plan to save the kingdom.

The next morning the King woke early and hurried down from the tower. When he arrived at the gates, he could see that a large crowd had gathered and everyone was excited about the weaver and his magic.

Moments later the weaver appeared, carrying his big brown sack. The crowd stepped aside as he made his way to the gates where the King waited.

The King, feeling the need to say something official, cleared his throat and spoke, "Loyal subjects, I give you the weaver." Before he could say more, everyone started cheering. The King raised one hand to silence the crowd and with the other he pointed to the big brown sack and asked, "Does this sack contain the magic that will stop the sadness and save my kingdom?"

Before the weaver could answer, the crowd cheered yet again. With that the King stepped back and commanded, "Let it begin!"

y now, the children had wiggled their way to the front of the crowd and formed a circle around the weaver and his leather sack. With eyes wide, not making a sound, they watched the weaver kneel down and open his sack.

Then he reached inside and gently pulled out a bright, red ribbon. It was the most beautiful ribbon anyone had ever seen, and it looked as if it could stretch for miles and miles and miles. The weaver then stood and held the ribbon high above his head.

"In order for the magic to work," he said, "you must do exactly as I say. This ribbon must be taken through the village, down the streets, through the alleys, and across the fields. You must take it throughout the kingdom, from the giant mountains to the great blue sea.

"Remember this! The ribbon must never touch the ground. Now listen very closely, for this is the most important part: everyone in the kingdom must share in this task. If anyone is left out, the magic will be broken, and the sadness will return."

Then the weaver took the end of the red ribbon and carefully placed it in the hands of a small boy standing at the front of the crowd. He told the boy to take the ribbon and lead the way throughout the kingdom.

After the boy had taken a few steps into the crowd, the weaver shouted, "Stop!" The crowd gasped as the boy froze. Looking back over his shoulder, the boy could see that if he took one more step the long ribbon would touch the ground. The crowd was silent.

The weaver said nothing. The King was speechless.

Then a tiny girl stepped out from the crowd, and reaching out her little hands, lifted the sagging red ribbon high above her head. Without a word she and the young boy turned and carried the ribbon forward.

ow everyone understood. One by one, the people of the
kingdom stepped forward to take their share of the
ribbon. The banker followed the carpenter, who followed
the schoolteacher, who followed the blacksmith. On and on they
came, to carry the bright, red ribbon throughout the kingdom.

Before long, hundreds of people were holding the ribbon.
It stretched from one corner of the kingdom to the other. They

held it high above their heads, just like the little girl, so that it would never touch the ground.

The King looked at the people and the ribbon stretching far into the distance. He looked at the leather sack, and then at the weaver. "So," he said, "when does the magic begin?"

"It has already begun," the weaver replied. And with that, he kindly took the King by the arm and led him along the great ribbon.

efore long they came to a young girl with the ribbon wrapped around her shoulders. She stood shivering in a thin and tattered dress. Next to her was a man in nice new clothes, who could not help but ask, "Where is your coat, young lady? It is much too cold to be without a coat!"

"I have no coat, sir," the girl said.

"No coat!" he exclaimed, waving his arms in the air. "Everyone should have a coat and that includes you."

ou see, I am a tailor. I make clothes
and I especially love making coats.
Why, I have dozens of coats in my shop. I have
green ones and orange ones, large
ones and small ones, and I'm
quite sure I have one just
right for you. It would make me

very happy to give you a coat to keep you warm."

The little girl smiled. The King was amazed. It was the first smile he'd seen in the kingdom in a long long time.

Even his frown was growing smaller.

"The magic is working," he thought. Then he turned to the weaver and said, "Please show me more."

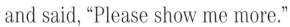

N ext, they came to a very thin old man. Beside him holding the ribbon was a round lady wearing a white apron and a floppy white hat.

"What is that growling?" the lady asked.

"Excuse me, ma'am," said the old man.

"That is my stomach. I hope it didn't frighten you."

"I've never heard such a growl from a tummy," the lady said. "Have you had nothing to eat today?"

"No," said the old man, "I've had no food for two days."

"Heavens!" she cried. "No food for two whole days? Why, I can go no more than two minutes without a little something to silence my tummy."

llow me to introduce myself. I am the village baker. If you come to my shop today, I'll fill your belly with warm bread and the finest cakes and pies in the kingdom."

"Thank you, kind lady. But I have no money," the old man said.

The baker thought for a moment. "My friend, I have an idea," she said. "I need someone to deliver my cakes and pies

to the townspeople. If you will help me, I'll pay you a fair wage. That way, you can buy food and we'll never hear your tummy complain again."

"I'll do it!" the old man said.

Again the King was amazed by what he heard. His frown almost vanished and he asked to see more.

oon they came to the crystal river where two men from different nations, standing tall and proud, held their share of the ribbon. Neither man said a word. In fact, they were trying very hard not to notice each other at all.

The men began to wonder how long they would have to stand there

holding the ribbon. "We may be side by side forever," each man thought. "Yet, I cannot let go of the ribbon. I will not be the one to break the magic."

As time passed the men realized their stubbornness was silly. If they were going to be together for a long time, it would be much easier to talk rather than to ignore each other. Finally, the silence was broken.

have noticed you have beautiful gardens on your side of the river," said one man. "You are quite a farmer. I would like to be able to grow vegetables like yours some day."

"Thank you," the farmer said. "I see you have built yourself quite a barn. You must have cut the wood from the tall trees that grow on your side of the river. You are quite a woodsman. I would like to have a barn like that some day."

The two men thought for a moment and then each man looked at the other.

"I have an idea," said the farmer. "I will give you some of my vegetables and teach you how to grow a garden like mine, if you will show me how to build a barn like yours."

"Show you how to build a barn!" exclaimed the woodsman. "I can do better than that.

Not only will I show you how, I will give you the wood with which to build it."

The two men didn't ignore each other any more.

That very day they built a bridge across the river so they could share with one another. The King was delighted with what he'd seen. His frown was completely gone and a big smile had taken its place.

The weaver and the King made their way throughout the entire kingdom. By now there was much celebration. People cheered, church bells rang, horns blew and at long last the King could hear the laughter of children. The sadness was gone! The kingdom was saved.

he King and the weaver returned to where it had all begun. Approaching the castle gates, they watched as the last person in the kingdom pulled the ribbon from the brown leather sack.

Suddenly. . .

the King began to panic! There was still more ribbon in the sack. "It must not touch the ground," he thought, and so he raced to catch it. Before he could reach the big brown sack, the last few feet of ribbon lifted out and fluttered in the breeze.

Slowly, very slowly, the red ribbon fell softly to the ground. The King dropped to his knees. His sad old frown returned. A tear puddled in his eye and rolled down his cheek. "The last hope to stop the sadness and save the kingdom is gone. What on earth will I do now?"

As the King stared at the ribbon lying on the ground, he noticed something. *Something wonderful.*

eople were cheering!
Bells were ringing!
Horns were blowing!
The children were laughing!
Though the ribbon had touched the
ground, the celebration had not stopped.

"The magic is still working!" the King
shouted as he jumped to his feet. "My dear
Weaver, your red ribbon is more
powerful and amazing than
even you imagined. You must tell
me how you made it. What is the
magic? Where does it come from?"

The weaver, saying nothing,
simply held out his hand and
pointed toward the people.

The King was puzzled. "I don't understand,"
he said. Then he looked out into the faces of
his people, and listened to their voices.

A big smile covered the
King's face as he realized,
"The magic is not in the
weaver's ribbon.

33

"he true magic is in the hands and hearts of those who embrace it."

And throughout the land, from the castle to the valley, from the crystal river to the big blue sea, one person turned to another, and another to another, with smiles on their faces and laughter in their voices. They sang and danced, knowing that the kingdom was saved and that as long as their hearts were joined together, they could conquer all sadness and live peacefully ever after.

The Beginning

The Storyteller:
John Lasne

Born on a small island off the coast of Charleston, South Carolina, John is a southern storyteller in the truest sense. He feels that the "art" of storytelling is more than just passing a story along. Most of the stories he tells are his own, and each has a message. The message might be serious or funny, sad or scary, but mostly it will be about life. When not telling stories, John carries mail for the U.S. Postal Service. John became involved with Red Ribbon through a Red Ribbon storytelling festival in 1992, shortly after which he created the story.

The Creative Team:
Brains on Fire

Brains on Fire specializes in strategic growth planning and creative resources. The company is headquartered in Greenville, South Carolina. Since 1991, Brains on Fire staff have worked creatively in drug prevention and produced the Red Ribbon poster which inspired John Lasne's story.

When John Lasne told his Red Ribbon story for the first time, Geno Church was in the audience. As the story unfolded, Geno saw its magic at work as people around him listened, enraptured. Geno, a volunteer with RRW and art director with Brains on Fire, knew the story would be a very special way to promote the Red Ribbon Campaign. His initial efforts led to the creation of *The Red Ribbon* storybook.

Greg Cordell and Greg Ramsey, partners in the firm, collaborated on *The Red Ribbon*. Cordell transformed the oral story into text and co-designed the book. A lifelong fan of Disney and a cartoonist at heart, he enjoyed bringing John Lasne's characters to life on the printed page, and believes strongly in the story's message of hope.

Greg Ramsey illustrated *The Red Ribbon*, inspired by works of the old masters and by his children, Morgan and Gregory. Ramsey has always loved children's books and was delighted to illustrate *The Red Ribbon*. "My motivation," he says, "was knowing that this story will help equip children for life. As I read it to my own children, I hope they embrace both its magic and its meaningful message."

The Red Ribbon, the partners' first collaboration on a storybook, is a wonderful, rich blend of Cordell's cartooning style and Ramsey's naturalistic attention to light, color and detail.

Pictured from front to back:
Greg Cordell, Greg Ramsey, Geno Church.